MUSEUM
MYSTERIES

Museum Mysteries is published by Stone Arch Books
A Capstone Imprint
1710 Roe Crest Drive
North Mankato, Minnesota 56003
www.mycapstone.com

Text and illustrations © 2019 Stone Arch Books

Library of Congress Cataloging-in-Publication Data is available
on the Library of Congress website.

ISBN: 978-1-4965-7817-4 (hardcover)
ISBN: 978-1-4965-8022-1 (paperback)
ISBN: 978-1-4965-7819-8 (eBook PDF)

Summary: The Capitol City Air and Space Museum is adding a new
exhibit, and Amal Farah and her friends get to attend the grand
opening! But before the new exhibit goes live, some of the items
go missing. Amal and her friends are determined to solve this crazy
mystery!

Design Elements by Shutterstock

Printed and bound in the USA.
PA49

The Case of the
EMPTY CRATES

By Steve Brezenoff
Illustrated by Lisa K. Weber

STONE ARCH BOOKS
a capstone imprint

Galileo's Telescope

- Galileo Galilei was an Italian physicist and astronomer. born in Pisa, Italy, in February 1564, Galileo is considered the father of modern science.

- Galileo was not the first person to invent the telescope. In 1608, eyeglass maker Hans Lippershey of Holland invented a "spyglass," patented as a "certain instrument for seeing far."

- Galileo's telescope, which improved upon the basic spyglass, was completed in 1609 and measured 36.5 inches long. It would become the prototype for the modern-day refractor telescope.

- One of Galileo's first discoveries was that the moon's surface was, "uneven, rough, full of cavities and prominences." Before his observations, people thought the moon was smooth and polished.

- At its strongest, Galileo's telescope was able to magnify things thirty times their normal size. In 1610, he used it to discover four new "stars" orbiting Jupiter—the planet's four largest moons.

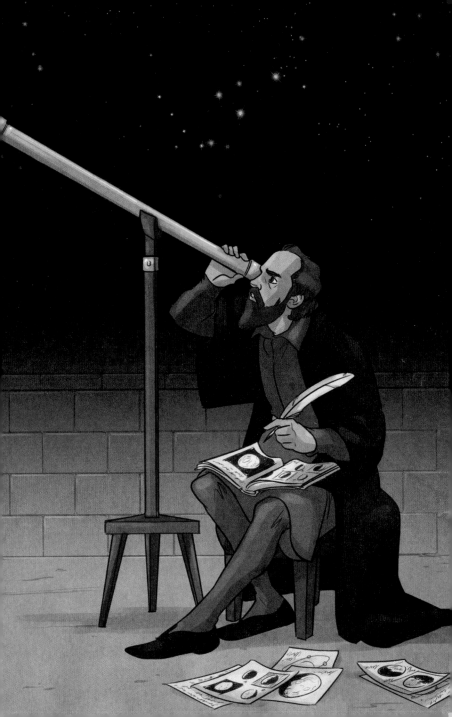

Amal Farah

Raining Sam

Wilson Kipper

Clementine Wim

Capitol City Sleuths

Amal Farah
Age: 11
Favorite Museum: Air and Space Museum
Interests: astronomy, space travel, and
building models of spaceships

Raining Sam
Age: 12
Favorite Museum: American History Museum
Interests: Ojibwe history, culture, and
traditions, American history — good and bad

Clementine Wim
Age: 13
Favorite Museum: Art Museum
Interests: painting, sculpting with clay, and
anything colorful

Wilson Kipper
Age: 10
Favorite Museum: Natural History Museum
Interests: dinosaurs (especially pterosaurs
and herbivores) and building dinosaur models

TABLE OF CONTENTS

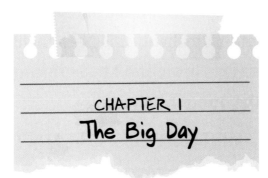

CHAPTER 1
The Big Day

Amal Farah paced the lobby of the Capitol City Air and Space Museum, where her father, Dr. Farah, was the head archivist. She was wearing her best clothes—a gold dress to match the golden stars of her favorite hijab.

Today was a very big day.

Dustin Stern, a local politician and millionaire, had donated a huge sum of money from his foundation to be used for a new wing at the Air and Space Museum. A luncheon was being held today so Dr. Farah and Mr. Stern could make the announcement.

"The luncheon begins soon," Dr. Farah said, glancing nervously at the time on his phone. "I need this to go smoothly. Where is Mr. Stern?"

"And where are my friends?" Amal asked. She knew her father was worried, but so was she. Her friends were late. For what felt like the tenth time, she stopped in front of the revolving doors and checked the drop-off circle. This time, an ancient-looking station wagon with fake wood paneling on its doors jerked to a stop in front.

"Finally!" Amal said. "They're here."
She pushed through the door. A gust of
misty rain swept her scarf and dress.

Clementine Wim, one of Amal's best
friends, climbed out of the front seat.
Clem wore a long silk dress decorated
with flowers from hem to neckline. Her
normally wild red hair was in a braided
bun today.

Amal's other two best friends, Raining
Sam and Wilson Kipper, climbed out of the
back seat. Both wore suits that didn't fit
quite right. Amal did her best not to laugh
at the boys looking very uncomfortable.

"I'm so glad you came!" Amal said.
"This is a big deal for my dad." She waved
goodbye to Clem's mom, Dr. Abigail Wim.

Dr. Wim was the assistant curator at the nearby Capitol City Art Museum. In fact, all the four friends' parents worked at one of the Capitol City museums, all adjacent to one another on Museum Circle.

"Have fun!" Clem's mom called as she drove off.

Amal ushered her friends inside, where her father was still waiting. Dr. Farah greeted them with a tense smile. He was clearly a bit worried about the luncheon ahead. Amal knew her father was under a lot of pressure from his boss to make the new wing a success.

"Is it true you've made Dustin Stern an honorary member of the museum staff?" Wilson asked.

Dr. Farah nodded, but he looked less than thrilled. "Indeed," he said.

"He's so lucky!" Wilson said. "Don't most of the staff have real expertise in some branch of the sciences?"

"That's true," Dr. Farah said. "Most of them have their doctorates. We've actually never made anyone an honorary staff member before."

"So why this time?" Amal asked. "I've been wondering."

"Mr. Stern insisted," Dr. Farah said with a shrug. "He said he's always wanted to be a staff member here. It was more important to him than what exhibit the wing would house. To make sure we got the donation, I hired him without pay."

"No pay?" Raining said. "He agreed to that?"

"Well, he's already a millionaire, for one thing," Dr. Farah said. "But mainly it's because honorary means we're honoring him. We're showing our appreciation for what he's done for the museum with the donation and new wing. It's not really a job."

"Can we go inside now?" Amal asked. She'd heard enough. She was excited to see how the Space Exploration Hall had been decked out for the luncheon.

"Sure, sure," Dr. Farah said. "You're at table number twelve."

"Come on, guys," Amal said. "See you later, Dad!"

Dr. Farah waved at her but kept his eyes on his phone. "Where *is* he?" he muttered.

Amal led her friends into the hall. The high ceiling was always something to behold: a powered mobile display of the entire Milky Way galaxy. It twinkled and swirled like a real night sky.

But today the hall was even more impressive than usual. It was filled with tables covered in white cloths. Each table had a fancy-looking bouquet of white flowers and was set with shining gold-and-white plates, glittering crystal glasses, and gold utensils.

At the front was a stage which held a podium and three big flat-screen displays.

Amal recognized some of the museum staff milling around, all dressed for the occasion. Her father's boss was there too, carefully observing. The catering staff—all in tuxedos—hurried to and fro, preparing for the lunch.

"Wow," Clementine said. "This is amazing. It's like a royal wedding in here."

The four kids found table twelve near the back of the hall and took their seats. They sat very still, all too nervous and excited to touch the fancy plates, forks, and glasses.

When Wilson took a sip from his water glass, the ice cubes clinked, breaking the silence. The friends all jumped and laughed.

Soon the other guests began to arrive. Many were familiar. There were lots of staff members from the Air and Space Museum, as well as representatives from the three nearby museums.

Suddenly Clementine waved at a woman wearing a green dress with a flared skirt and a whisper-thin scarf tied around her neck. The young woman waved back and came over to their table. She didn't look happy.

"Who's that?" Amal asked.

"That's Bridget Byrne," Clementine said. "She's one of the youngest people in the Art Museum's fundraising and promotion office. I've met her there a couple times. She comes to a lot of parties and dinners and stuff like this on behalf of the museum."

"Hi, Clementine," Bridget said, slumping into an empty seat at their table.

"Hey, Bridget," Clem replied. "How's it going?"

Bridget sighed. "I wish I could sit back here with you kids where no one could see me," she said. "I'm just in no mood for a donation announcement today."

"What's wrong?" Clem asked.

"Oh, same old thing," Bridget said, sitting up. "Museum funds are thinner than the fabric of my scarf."

The hall began to fill up.

"I'd better find my seat," Bridget said as she stood. "Have fun, kids. See you, Clementine."

Once everyone was seated, Dr. Farah took the stage and tapped the microphone.

"Thank you all for coming," he said. "We'll just have a short program before lunch is served. As you know, councilman Dustin Stern, also a great philanthropist, has recently made a significant donation to the Capitol City Air and Space Museum."

At that, the screens behind Dr. Farah switched on, showing a photo of the museum.

"With his generous assistance," Dr. Farah continued, "we're pleased to announce today that we are nearing completion on the new Dustin Stern Wing!"

The screens onstage faded to black and then showed a digital version of what the completed wing would look like.

The crowd *oohed* and *ahhed*, then burst into applause.

"To tell us more about it," Dr. Farah said as the clapping quieted, "here is councilman, businessman, and the newest *honorary* member of museum staff, Dustin Stern himself!"

Dustin Stern rose from his seat and took the stage. He wore a white linen shirt, dark linen pants, and expensive-looking eyeglasses. His dark hair was brushed back from his forehead and slicked down with hair gel.

"I guess he showed up after all," Amal whispered to Raining.

"Thank you all so much for joining us today," Mr. Stern said after shaking Dr. Farah's hand. "I couldn't be happier about this project. But I don't see my donation as supporting the museum—not exactly."

Amal and her friends exchanged confused looks.

"To me, that money will support the visitors who come to this museum once the new wing is complete," Mr. Stern continued. "The families, the children, the school field trips—those are the people my foundation and I are giving this money.

"Because after all," he concluded, "if we can't support, educate, and inspire our children, where do we stand as a society?"

The room erupted into tremendous applause. The guests rose to their feet and cheered.

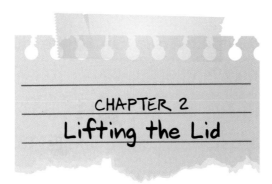

CHAPTER 2
Lifting the Lid

"Everyone, please put on a hard hat!"
Dr. Farah called. "That's the rule!"

The luncheon guests, including Amal and
her friends, gathered outside the gated-off,
nearly complete new wing. Everyone looked
funny wearing their fancy clothes with a
bright-orange hard hat on top.

"And now for our tour of the new wing,"
Dr. Farah announced, his hands clasped

together. "This is a very important addition to our museum. One I am so very proud to oversee. But for the tour, Mr. Stern will take the lead."

The guests followed as the gate was opened, and Dustin Stern and Dr. Farah went inside. Though the wing was incomplete—not even connected to the main building yet—the sign had already been erected:

WELCOME TO THE DUSTIN STERN WING
EXPLORING THE UNIVERSE
FROM HERE AT HOME

In smaller gold print, it read:

HOUSING THE EARLIEST DEVICES FOR OBSERVATION AND
THE MOST POWERFUL TELESCOPES OF TODAY—AND
TOMORROW

Beyond that, the wing was basic. It had a ceiling and walls and a floor. Some of the display furnishings—like pedestals, cases, and guardrails—had already been installed. Wooden crates of all sizes—at least twenty of them—were scattered around. Each one was labeled FRAGILE and addressed to the museum, stamped by the Hardison Shipping Company.

"They sure put this together quickly," Raining said. "We were sitting on the grass right here a couple weeks ago."

Dustin Stern overheard and turned to face them. "I pulled some strings," he said, smiling.

"What's in all the crates?" Clementine asked. "More construction equipment?"

Mr. Stern laughed. "No, no," he said. "Those are the items that will be on display here in the Dustin Stern Wing. They're quite fragile—and valuable. So please don't touch."

"What kind of things?" Wilson asked.

"Um . . . let me think," Mr. Stern said, studying the crates. "This shipment arrived last night. I think it was . . . yes, that's right. Antique telescopes from Europe. From the seventeenth and eighteenth centuries."

"Wow!" Amal said, her eyes wide. "I wonder if one of Galileo's telescopes is in here."

"I'm afraid I have no idea," Mr. Stern said curtly. He walked off to continue leading the tour. A moment later he could be heard talking about where the bathrooms would be.

"The finest toilet bowls money can buy!" he said, thrusting a finger into the air. The guests cheered.

Dr. Farah brought up the rear of the tour. "Hey, kids," he said. "Better keep up. I can't stay back and keep an eye on you. Not with Mr. Stern and my boss here."

"Aw, Dad," Amal said. "We don't want to hear Dustin Stern talk anymore. We just want to look around."

Dr. Farah frowned. "OK," he said. "But stay out of trouble. And stay out of the way. And don't touch anything! I can't afford to have anything broken."

With that, he hurried away to catch up with the tour.

Left on their own, Amal and her friends wandered among the crates, studying the labels to see what might be inside. The labels, though, gave away nothing.

"I have to open one," Amal said. "I have to know what's inside!"

"Geez, Amal," Raining said. "I know you like astronomy, but I've never heard of anyone this excited about some old telescopes."

"You know who would have been this excited?" Amal said, her enthusiasm unwavering. "The astronomers from Galileo's and Isaac Newton's time."

"How do you know?" Wilson said, crossing his arms.

"Because Isaac Newton built the first telescope with a reflector," Amal said. "Not to mention everything he did for astrophysics. And Galileo is credited with being the first person to ever point a telescope into space. He drew detailed pictures of the moon. They're famous."

"He drew pictures?" Clementine said. Her interest peaked at the mention of artwork. "Are they in one of these boxes?"

Amal's eyes went wide. "Maybe!" she said. "See? That's why I want to poke around a little. I can't wait to see this stuff."

"That's not fair," Clementine said. "If they're drawings, they should be next door in the Art Museum."

"Come on," Amal said, ignoring Clem's comment. She ran to a box about waist height. "This one we can probably open."

"Amal!" Raining said. "You heard what your dad said. Don't touch anything."

"I'm not going to touch anything *inside*," Amal insisted. "I'll just open this and peek in. Whatever's in there, I will not touch."

She pulled at the lid. It didn't budge.

"It's nailed on," she said, disappointed.

"Oh well," Raining said. "No rule breaking today, I guess."

"I'll help," Clementine offered. "I want to see if those drawings are in there. There has to be a tool around here somewhere."

Clementine poked around and found a toolbox that had been left behind from construction. She returned carrying a couple of hammers.

Together the two girls pried at the lid. Slowly the nails lifted out of the wood. Then suddenly the lid popped off and clattered to the ground.

"I hope no one heard that," Wilson said.

The four friends waited quietly, sure they'd hear the sound of footsteps—angry adult ones—hurrying toward them. But after a moment, the coast was still clear.

Amal looked into the box. It was full
of shredded paper and packing material.
She reached in and felt around.

"Hey!" Raining said, grabbing her arm.
"You said you wouldn't touch anything."

Amal pulled away from her friend's grasp. "And I didn't touch anything," she said. "Because there's nothing in there to touch."

"Huh?" Clementine said. She joined Amal at the edge of the box and reached both hands in. There was nothing but shredded paper and packing peanuts inside. "That's weird."

"No, it's not," Wilson said. He picked up the lid and gently pushed the girls aside. "They probably already unpacked everything." He turned to Raining. "Help me put this back on."

The boys got the lid into positin and knocked the nails back in place as best they could.

"If the crates have already been unpacked, then where is everything?" Amal asked, looking around.

"In storage?" Wilson said. "I bet your dad would know."

Amal shook her head. "No way," she said. "If my dad had unpacked any old telescopes, he would have told me. He knows how interested I am in that stuff."

"Maybe he's not the one who unpacked them," Wilson said.

"OK," Amal went on, "say it was someone else. Who unloads a crate, closes it back up, and leaves it on the floor of the new wing they're about to show off to the entire cultural society of Capitol City? It makes no sense."

Raining glanced at Wilson. They both shrugged. "Maybe," they said.

"Looks like we have a mystery to solve," Amal said. "Whether you want to believe it or not."

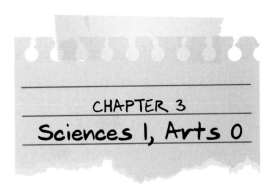

CHAPTER 3
Sciences 1, Arts 0

"I still say this is a waste of time," Amal said as she and her friends hurried through the construction zone to find the tour and Dr. Farah. "My dad would have told me if he'd opened any of the crates for the new wing."

"There they are," Clementine said, pointing. As the tallest of their group of friends, she often was first to spot

whatever—or whoever—they happened
to be looking for.

"Dad!" Amal said, hurrying to the
back of the tour. "About the crates back
there, I—"

"Just a second," Dr. Farah said
into his cellphone. He covered the
mouthpiece. "Amal, I'm on the phone.
I cannot help you and your friends
today. It's a busy day, you know that.
I have a lot riding on this exhibit, and
there's so much to do. Mr. Stern is a very
important guest."

"I know," Amal said, "but, Dad. This
is important. We—"

"Not now," Dr. Farah said firmly.
He put the phone back to his ear.

"Now then, about Mr. Stern's dinner reservations, he wants a table near the north window, and . . ."

"Did you hear that?" Amal said as she rejoined her friends. "Dad wouldn't even let me ask him about the empty crate. He's too busy making dinner reservations for Mr. Stern."

She stood with her friends, sulking, as the tour moved on.

"Don't look so down," Bridget, the Art Museum staff member, said. She stood alone near a pile of crates in the corner. As Amal watched, she brushed a bit of what looked like a packing peanut off her skirt. "Your dad's doing what any good museum rep would do in this situation."

"What do you mean?" Clementine asked.

"Dustin Stern is probably the most important donor the Air and Space Museum has had since it was founded," Bridget said. "Dr. Farah is doing everything he can to make sure his biggest donor is happy."

"I guess that makes sense," Amal said. She moved to stand next to Bridget. "But my dad is a doctor. He's super smart about astronomy and information technology and archives. He shouldn't have to be some rich guy's errand boy. I don't like it."

"And he shouldn't have to make Mr. Stern a member of the staff," Wilson added. "I got the impression your dad wasn't super into the idea. He said Mr. Stern insisted."

Bridget looked toward where the rest of the tour had gathered. The group was standing near a large window at the end of the wing. Beyond that was the Capitol City Art Museum.

"Look at that," she said. "The Air and Space Museum is now practically touching the Art Museum. Pretty soon we'll have to pick up the whole Art Museum and move it so Air and Space can have more room."

"Oh, come on," Clementine said. "That would never happen."

"Maybe," Bridget said with a shrug. "Maybe not. But the Art Museum has been eyeing the land just outside its Old Masters room for years—the land we're sitting on right now, under this new floor. Now it'll never be ours."

"Oh," Clementine said. "That is too bad. The Art Museum could use more space."

"Why is that too bad?" Amal said. She crossed her arms, still angry at her father and now feeling defensive about the Air and Space Museum being attacked. "We got the donor, so we get the land and the new wing. Seems fair to me."

"Maybe," Bridget said. "But take it from someone who spends every hour of every day hunting down donors for the arts. Money flows into the sciences from all over—corporations, government groups, even private donors like Dustin Stern. The arts are left begging for scraps, and it's never enough."

"Sounds like sour grapes," Amal said. With that, she stormed off toward the main part of the museum.

"Well, she's not wrong," Bridget said. "These grapes are so sour they're practically vinegar. See you around, Clementine." With that, she headed off to rejoin the tour.

"Come on," Raining said. "We'd better go after Amal."

CHAPTER 4
Splitting Up

Raining, Wilson, and Clementine found Amal sitting near the lunar lander. She was looking at her phone.

"Took you guys long enough," Amal said."

"Us?" Raining said. "You're the one who stomped off all angry."

Raining and Amal had been friends for a long time. In fact, Raining had been

Amal's first friend in Capitol City. He knew it would be OK to call her on her sudden bad mood.

"What are you looking at?" Clementine asked, trying to change the subject. She peeked over Amal's shoulder at her phone.

"I'm googling Bridget Byrne," Amal replied.

"Bridget?" Clem repeated, looking confused. "Why?"

"Isn't it obvious?" Amal said. "An entire crate worth of pieces is missing from the new wing. Bridget was standing right by the crates when we caught up to the tour. Didn't you see her brush that packing material off her skirt?"

"Oh, come on," Wilson interrupted. "First of all, we don't know there's actually anything missing. You're overreacting. And second of all, the wing is still under construction. Her having something stuck to her skirt doesn't prove anything."

Amal glared at him a moment, clearly not happy to be contradicted. Then she went on, "And we know one person who is especially upset about the new wing."

"You?" Raining said.

"Me?" Amal repeated. "I'm thrilled about the new wing."

"Then why are you in such a bad mood all of a sudden?" he asked.

"Because *some* people seem to think the Art Museum should be getting a new wing instead of the Air and Space Museum," Amal said, glaring at Clementine now.

"What?" Clementine said. "Amal, I never said that. I was just—"

"Save it!" Amal said, holding up a hand. "I'm researching the number-one suspect in the theft of those pieces: your friend Bridget Byrne."

"That's ridiculous!" Clementine said, stomping one foot. "Bridget would never do something like that. Just because she loves the Art Museum doesn't mean she wants to harm *this* museum."

"Oh, you know her so well?" Amal said. "Is she your best friend?"

"No!" Clementine said. "You are.
The three of you are my best friends."

"Right," Amal said. "That's why you
took Bridget's side just now."

"I did not!" Clementine said, looking at the boys for support. "I just said the Art Museum could use more space."

"Maybe you're in on it with her," Amal said. She crossed her arms.

Clementine tightened her fists at her sides. She clenched her jaw. Then without a word, she turned and stormed away.

"Umm," Wilson said after a moment of silence. "I'll find her." He ran off after Clementine.

"That's fine," Amal said. "We don't need them. We can solve this crime on our own."

Raining sighed. "If this even is a crime."

"Just trust me," Amal said.

"Fine," Raining said. "But when we prove you're wrong about Clementine you're going to owe her a big apology. Where do we start?"

CHAPTER 5
Mr. Not-So-Nice Guy

"There's just no talking to Amal when she gets like this!" Clementine said to Wilson as they walked through the hall where the luncheon had been held. The tables had been cleared away. Workers were now folding and removing the last sections of the stage. "It's so frustrating! How could she say that to me?"

Wilson patted her on the back. "Don't worry," he said. "She'll come around. She knows we're all best friends."

At the other side of the hall, Dustin Stern was taking a call on his cell phone.

"There he is," Clementine said. "The man of the hour."

"Can you imagine having the money he has?" Wilson asked.

"I sure can," Clementine said with a smile. "I dream about being a millionaire, like, every day."

"You do?" Wilson said. He shot his friend a surprised look. He knew Clementine extremely well, and he'd never heard her say anything about money. "But you're . . . you're . . ."

"What?" Clementine said, putting her fists on her hips. "An artist? A hippie?"

"I didn't say that," Wilson said. "You're just . . . not super into material things."

"That's true," Clementine admitted. "And the things I do have are pretty old, or used, or for my paintings or sculpture."

"So what's the million bucks for?" Wilson asked.

"To buy art supplies!" Clementine said. "That stuff is expensive."

"Ah," Wilson said with a laugh. That sounded more like the Clem he knew and loved.

"Besides," Clementine went on, "after this morning, I'd probably give the million bucks to the Art Museum."

"That would solve everything," Wilson said.

"Hey, you kids better clear out," one of the workers told them. "We're going to run the floor buffer in a minute."

"OK," Wilson said. He and Clementine headed for the exit. They passed Dustin Stern on their way out.

"Look, I don't care what it takes," Mr. Stern snarled into the phone. "Turn off the power if you have to. But get those people *out*. I want that property on the market first thing Monday morning."

He clicked off the call and shoved the phone into his pocket. Then he turned and saw the kids. For a moment,

he seemed surprised and irritated, but he recovered quickly.

"That's life in the real estate business, you know," Mr. Stern said. He winked at them and walked off as the floor buffer turned on.

"He's not the nice man he seemed at the lectern today, is he?" Clementine said when they were a few steps away.

"I guess he's pretty cutthroat about business," Wilson said. "I don't know any businesspeople. Maybe that's how you make it to the top. He sure has."

"I guess," Clementine said. "Still, which Mr. Stern is real? The one who talked about education and inspiration for children and families at museums?

Or the one who just said to get people out of a property so he could sell it?"

"I don't know," Wilson said. "But just knowing there's a different side to him makes the money for the wing seem a little . . ."

He trailed off, but Clementine knew what he was thinking. "Dirty," she finished.

CHAPTER 6
A Whole Lot of Nothing

In the new wing, the tour was over, the guests were gone, and the construction crew was getting ready for an afternoon of hard work. Amal and Raining had the place mostly to themselves.

"This way," Amal said. She led Raining around the gated area and through the side door into the new wing.

"I don't think we're supposed to be here," Raining said.

"Oh, come on," Amal said. "I'm not going to do anything this time."

"It's dark," he said, peering around the empty wing. "Are you sure it's safe?"

"Are you afraid of the dark now?" Amal said.

"Not the dark," Raining said. "But I am afraid of bits of the building falling on my head."

"Here," Amal said. She took two hard hats out of a bin near the door they'd come in through. "Put this on."

Both now wearing safety gear, they walked slowly through the darkened section of the new wing. Wires dangled from the ceiling where tiles hadn't been installed yet.

Raining kicked at the cement that was exposed where carpet hadn't been laid yet. Dust flew up from the toe of his sneaker.

"This place is falling apart," he said, "and it's not even together yet."

"Look at this," Amal said. "I found another crate. Come help me open it."

"Amal!" Raining complained. "You just said you weren't going to do anything this time."

"Just one crate," she said. "It's part of our investigation."

"How?" Raining said. "How is opening another crate going to help us find out

who robbed the first crate. If someone even did?"

"Simple," Amal said. "Wilson and Clementine don't believe something was stolen. They think the crate was empty because it was already unpacked. If *this* one is full, it will prove they haven't unpacked yet."

"Which means something really was stolen out of the first crate," Raining concluded.

"Exactly," Amal said.

"OK, fine," he said. "I'll help you. Last time, though."

"Deal," Amal said. "On three."

They both grabbed hold of the crate's heavy lid.

"One, two, *three!*" Amal said, and together they wrenched the lid off.

"Now let's see," Amal said. She leaned way over the edge of the crate. This one was a little bigger than the first. In fact, she could have probably climbed right in and packed herself if she'd wanted to.

"Anything?" Raining asked.

"Yeah, loads of stuff," Amal said. "Shredded paper, packing peanuts, torn newspaper . . ."

"So loads of nothing," Raining said.

"Exactly," Amal said.

Together they put the lid back on and secured it as well as they could.

"So maybe they're all unpacked already," Raining said.

Amal shook her head. "It can't be," she said. "I know you guys all think I'm making up a crime where there isn't one, but something's fishy. I know it. And I think the Capitol City Art Museum and Bridget Byrne are behind it."

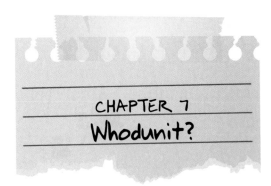

CHAPTER 7
Whodunit?

Amal led Raining through the museum at a fast pace, heading back toward the main entrance.

"Could you slow down a little?" Raining asked, a little short of breath. "Your legs are longer than mine, you know. What's the rush?"

"Are you kidding?" Amal said. "We're on a major case. If the new Dustin Stern

Wing opens and there are no exhibits, it could ruin the museum *and* my dad."

"So where are we going?" Raining said.

"To find Clementine," Amal replied. "Obviously."

"Oh!" Raining said, smiling. "That's good. I'm glad you two are going to make up and work on the case together."

"Work on the case—" Amal started. "No, that's not why—oh, here she comes now."

"Hello, Amal," Clementine said coolly.

Wilson stood at her side. "Clementine is very upset," he said to Amal.

"*She's* upset?" Amal said. "Do you know what Raining and I just discovered?"

Wilson and Clementine looked at Raining.

"Hey, whoa," he said, holding up his hands. "Let her tell you."

Amal glared at Raining. Then, with a huff, she told Clementine and Wilson about the second empty crate they'd just discovered.

"In other words," she finished, "this is a greater crime than I first realized. We don't know how many crates are empty. But at least two precious items are missing from the new collection."

"OK . . . ," Clementine said slowly. "Say this is a crime. Why would someone want whatever was inside those crates? What's the motive?"

"Because whatever was inside is valuable," Amal said. "Why else would someone steal it? You said yourself the Art Museum needs more money, right?"

"What are you saying?" Clementine said, crossing her arms.

"I think you know," Amal said, crossing her arms too. "Your best friend Bridget Byrne probably set it up because she's jealous. After all, she's in charge of raising money for the Art Museum."

"That's ridiculous!" Clementine protested. She was almost on the verge of tears now.

"And meanwhile," Amal continued, seeming like she might cry too, "when this new exhibit is ruined because of the theft, my dad will probably be out of a job!"

Clementine stomped the floor and clenched her teeth. "You're unbelievable!" she said, glaring at Amal. When Wilson made a move toward her, she snapped. "Don't follow me!"

With that, Clementine stormed off, right through the revolving doors and out of the museum.

"What is your problem?" Wilson said to Amal. He shoved his hands into the pockets of his fancy dress pants. "Ease up on her a little!"

"Ease up?" Amal repeated. "How can you say that to me? She keeps defending the thief!"

"You don't *know* that Bridget is the thief," Raining pointed out.

"Well she's definitely the number-one suspect," Amal argued.

"Only according to you," Wilson said. "And if we do find proof that she is behind the empty crate, you know Clem won't take her side. She's our best friend—*your* best friend."

Amal took a deep breath. Maybe the boys had a point. But she was too focused on solving the case to admit it. "Are we done?" she said. "Because we have more sleuthing to do."

With a last glance out the door Clementine had disappeared through, the boys followed Amal. She led the way toward her father's office. By now, he'd probably be done catering to Dustin Stern's every whim.

As they approached the doorway, though, they could hear Dr. Farah's voice. He didn't sound happy.

"Uh-oh," Amal said, grabbing the boys' wrists to stop them from going into the office.

The three snoopers stood outside the open door, hidden from view, and listened.

"You're going to tell me," Dr. Farah shouted, "that you delivered an *empty* crate to this museum—a crate that weighed almost nothing but was large enough to hold both of you—and that didn't seem strange?"

"I guess your dad found one of the empty crates," Raining whispered.

"And I guess they weren't unpacked," Wilson added. "That answers that question at least."

"Shh," Amal hissed at both of them.

"Look, dude," said another voice. "We don't inspect the packages. We just work for Hardison Shipping. They put the crates on our truck, and we drive them where they tell us to drive them."

"Why would we order an empty crate?" Dr. Farah shouted. "It was full of nothing but stuffing and foam peanuts!"

"So take it up with the sender, not the shipping company!" another man replied.

Suddenly the shouting stopped. From inside the office, footsteps came toward the door. Amal, Raining, and Wilson hurried around the corner. They watched Dr. Farah's office as two men in brown uniforms exited, looking as angry as they had sounded.

"Let's go talk to your dad," Raining said.

Amal shook her head. "No way," she said. "He's in no mood right now. Besides, he obviously has no idea why the crates are empty. We should follow the delivery guys. Come on."

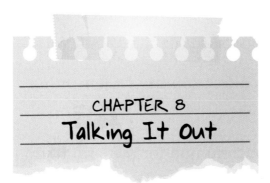

CHAPTER 8
Talking It Out

Clementine sat on the curb of the
pickup circle in front of the Capitol City
Air and Space Museum. She wished
she'd brought her sketch book along.
She also wished she wasn't wearing a
dress that made sitting on the curb quite
so awkward.

"Is this seat taken?" someone asked
softly.

Clementine looked up. Bridget Byrne stood over her, partially blocking out the afternoon sun.

"It's a free country," Clementine muttered.

"Good enough for me," said Bridget. She sat down on the curb next to Clementine. "Wanna talk about it?"

"About what?" Clementine said. She leaned her elbows on her knees and put her face in her hands.

"Come on," Bridget said, giving her a little shove. "I was there earlier, remember? Your friend didn't exactly seem happy. Are you two fighting?"

Clementine nodded. "Well," she said, "she's still fighting with me, anyway."

"Go on," Bridget said.

"Amal is convinced that everyone who has anything to do with the Art Museum simply *hates* the Air and Space Museum," Clementine said. "Including me." She turned toward Bridget. "And you!"

"Me?" Bridget said. She looked surprised for a moment. "Well, I can understand why she might think that. I was a little bitter about the new wing earlier."

"*And* she thinks you stole some valuable pieces from the new wing," Clementine added quietly.

"Me?" Bridget said again, looking truly shocked now. "I would never do that to the museum. Heck, I've never stolen anything in my life." She looked thoughtful for a moment. "Well, technically there was a piece of chewing gum once. . . . I took it out of a jar at the vet's office. I think they were free, but I didn't check first. It's been bugging me ever since."

"Be serious!" Clementine said.

"OK, OK," Bridget said. "Sorry. How can I help?"

"Maybe tell Amal that you had nothing do with any theft?" Clementine said. "Maybe she'll believe you more than she believes me."

"Sure," Bridget said with a shrug. "Be happy to." She stood and offered Clementine a hand. "Come on. Let's find her right now."

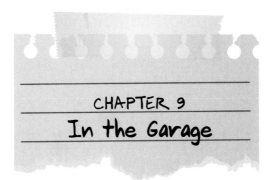

CHAPTER 9
In the Garage

Amal, Raining, and Wilson followed the two men wearing brown delivery uniforms. They were big, tough-looking guys—strong enough to carry huge boxes—so the three young sleuths stayed well back from them.

"It looks like they're heading for the loading bay in back," Amal said. "What could they be up to?"

"Probably loading," Wilson said.

"Or unloading," Raining added.

Amal rolled her eyes. "Shh," she said. "Listen."

The kids came to a strop behind a wide column in the high-ceilinged garage. The loading bay doors were both fully open. Two brown shipping-company trucks sat idle in the garage. A man in tan pants, a white shirt, and a loose black tie leaned against one truck and looked at his phone.

The two burly men approached him.

"Hey, Bruno," said one of the deliverymen.

The man looked up from his phone. "Hiya, Jimmy," he said. He looked at the other deliveryman and added, "Rocky, what's the situation?"

"Dr. Farah thinks something's up," Rocky replied. "He's mad about a couple of the deliveries from early this morning."

Bruno put his phone away and crouched to the pavement. He set down his briefcase and popped open the top.

"I'll handle Dr. Farah," Bruno said, looking inside. "I've got the solution right here."

Amal gasped. From where she, Wilson, and Raining were standing, they couldn't see inside. But whatever "the solution" was, it didn't sound good.

"We have to warn your dad," Raining said. "Right now."

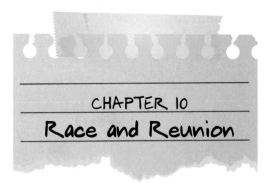

CHAPTER 10
Race and Reunion

Amal, Raining, and Wilson sprinted through the museum's hallways. They couldn't risk using the back way—that was the most logical route for Bruno to take from the loading docks.

They definitely didn't want to run into him on the way to Dr. Farah's office.

As they zoomed through the hall, with its freshly buffed wood floors, they slipped

and careened into one another—then into Clementine and Bridget, who were hurrying in the opposite direction. The five of them ended up tumbled in a pile in the middle of the hall.

"Amal," Clementine said. "We've been looking for you."

Amal glanced quickly at Clementine, and then shot Bridget a withering glare. "Whatever it is, I don't have time right now," she said. "My dad is in danger."

With that, she took off running again. Raining and Wilson hurried after her.

Clementine followed, and Bridget had to run to catch up. "Wait for me!"

Amal sneakers skidded and squeaked as she stopped just inside the doorway to her father's office. She was always the fastest, and right now her father's life might depend on her.

But she was too late. Bruno was already there.

Dr. Farah stood behind his desk, obviously angry. Bruno set the briefcase down on the desk and reached for the clasps.

"Dad!" Amal shouted. "In the briefcase. He—"

Bruno popped the leather case open and pulled out a long, yellow sheet of paper.

"Oh," Amal said. "Never mind."

The two men looked at her a moment.

"Anyway," Bruno said, "as you see here—"

"It just doesn't make sense," Dr. Farah cut him off. "My people are still going through the crates, but so far all we've found are two dozen crates full of nothing but packing material! What happened to the pieces that should be in there?"

"That's what I'm trying to tell you," Bruno said, poking the yellow paper with one stubby finger. "I have your order right here. Look for yourself."

"Give me that," Dr. Farah said, snatching the paper from Bruno. He scanned the paper, running a finger down the list as he went.

Amal watched as her father's face went from fuming angry to totally confused to deeply depressed.

"Dad?" Amal said, stepping a little farther into the room. "What is it?"

Dr. Farah handed the paper back to Bruno, sat in his desk chair, and put his head on the desk.

"It's like I said," Bruno said. "The order is very specific: twenty crates of different volumes, all full of packing material and nothing else."

Bruno showed Amal the paper. He was right.

"But this makes no sense," Amal said.

Bruno gave a big shrug. "What do I know?" he said. "I'm just the delivery guy." With that, he closed the briefcase and left the office.

"Dad, how could this be?" Amal asked.

Dr. Farah rolled his head side to side on the desk. "I can't understand it," he mumbled to no one in particular. "I should have checked the crates the moment they arrived. We have less than two weeks until the wing is supposed to open. It's ruined. *I'm* ruined. My career is over!"

CHAPTER 11
Follow the Money

"Um, we'll give you some space, Dr. Farah," Bridget said. She ushered the four friends quietly out of the room.

But as soon as the five of them stepped into the hallway, Amal jerked her arm away. "Don't touch me!" she snapped at Bridget.

"Amal!" Clementine said. "That is enough! You're being ridiculous. Bridget and I don't have anything to do with the empty crates!"

"Well, I think you do," Amal said. "Who else has a motive to hate the new wing?"

"I don't hate the new wing," Clementine insisted.

"*She* does," Amal said. She crossed her arms and glared at Bridget.

"I don't *hate* it either," Bridget said. "I resent it a little, but . . ."

Amal sneered at her.

"Look, Amal," Bridget said. "Do you think Clementine or Dr. Wim or I got interested in art or started working with it for the money?"

Amal shrugged.

"Well, we didn't," Bridget said. "Art is simply the most important thing in our lives, maybe second only to family."

"So?" Amal said. "Science and museums are like that for my dad."

"Exactly," Bridget said. "We're all very lucky, because we get to work in a field that we truly love. But that doesn't mean we'd break the law, or take something that wasn't ours, or try to ruin another person's passion. Science is super important too, even if it doesn't happen to be the field that *we* love."

"And you have to know I'd never be involved with anything that might hurt your father," Clementine said. "Or you."

Amal nodded and looked at her feet, a little ashamed that she'd been so hard on her friend. She'd just been so worried about her father and caught up in solving the case.

"Do I resent the money that sciences get over the arts?" Bridget said. "Sure I do. I get a little tired of always coming in second—"

"Or third or fourth," Clementine interjected.

"—in the eyes of local politicians who decide where funds go," Bridget finished.

"Politicians like Mr. Stern," Amal added.

"Yup," Bridget said. "Heck, he's a politician and millionaire rolled into one."

"And a real estate magnate," Wilson added.

Bridget nodded. "He gets to decide about *lots* of money and where it'll go," she said.

"That's right," Clementine agreed. "I have a feeling *his* passion is money itself. Remember? We heard him on the phone."

"He sounded like he might do anything for land or money—or both," Wilson said.

Clementine thought for a moment. "You're right," she said. "He *did* sound like he'd do anything, hurt anyone. He said talking like that was how people made it in the business world, but maybe it wasn't just talk."

"Wait a minute," Amal said. She turned to Bridget. "You said the Art Museum was looking at the plot of land that one end of the new wing is on, right?"

Bridget nodded. "It was way out of our price range, though," she admitted. "I tried so hard to get donations. We did a few mailings. My whole staff was on the phone for weeks, but it just wasn't enough."

"Who was selling it?" Amal asked, suddenly curious.

Bridget thought for a moment. "A realty firm," she said. "I think it was called Bright Star. Or Brave Star maybe? I can't remember."

"Huh," Wilson said. "That's funny. Did you know *stern* is the German word for *star*? I learned that in school last year."

"As in Dustin Stern?" Amal said.

Wilson nodded and pulled out his phone. "And you know what else?" he said, looking at his screen. He held it up so everyone could see the results. "According to this website, the name Dustin means 'brave or valiant fighter.'"

"Brave Star," Amal concluded. "I think we've cracked this. Let's go get my dad."

CHAPTER 12
Closing In

"You're sure you saw him heading toward the exit?" Amal shouted. Her friends, her father, and Bridget Byrne ran after her through the museum's front lobby.

Dr. Farah nodded, out of breath. "Def-definitely," he huffed. "He said he had an important meeting that he can't miss."

"There he is!" Clementine announced. She pointed through the glass doors toward the parking lot.

Together the group burst through the side doors and raced toward Mr. Stern. Clementine and Amal ran side by side.

"Hey," Amal said as they ran across the parking lot. "I'm sorry. I shouldn't have accused you. I should have trusted you."

"Thanks," Clementine said. They paused to hug briefly, then picked up the pace again.

"Now let's get him," Amal said, slowing down a bit so they could approach quietly.

Mr. Stern stood next to his open car door with his phone to his ear. He leaned against the car, his back to the group.

"Nah," he said to whoever was on the phone. "It's junk construction. Shoddy materials, hollow posts, windows with no glass . . . It cost us pennies. All I had to do was ship some empty crates to make it look like we were really planning to stock the wing. They didn't even check them."

"What is he talking about?" Dr. Farah whispered to his daughter as they eavesdropped on the phone call.

"The new wing," Amal said. "And doing anything and hurting anyone. Whatever he has to do just to make a good real estate deal."

"I'm telling you," Mr. Stern went on, "the condos we'll build on the property when this is all finished is well worth it. We're going to make back the money we spent on the museum land *and* the money we sank into this phony new wing, plus another ten million on top of that. Trust me!"

Mr. Stern turned around, wearing a big smile on his face. But when he saw Dr. Farah, the smile dropped away.

"Uh, let me call you back," he said, quickly hanging up the phone. "Dr. Farah, about what you just heard . . ."

"Save it," Amal said, stepping right up to him.

Mr. Stern backed away a few steps.

"We know exactly what you've been up to, Mr. Stern," she said. "Or should I call you Brave Star?"

Mr. Stern's eyes went wide.

"You donated money from your foundation," Amal said, "and then used that money to buy land from your own real estate company."

"Well, I am a shareholder," Mr. Stern replied.

"And now," Amal continued, "you're planning to knock the wing down and build condos."

"But you can't do that," Dr. Farah said. "The land isn't zoned for residential use. Besides, the museum owns the land."

"And I am an employee of the museum," Mr. Stern said. "You helped me with that."

"An honorary employee," Dr. Farah said. "And employees don't have the right to just sell off pieces of the museum's land."

"No, but I do," Mr. Stern said. "I was very careful with the wording of the contract *you* signed for my new position."

"But that still won't help you with the zoning issue," Raining pointed out.

"Ah, but it will," Mr. Stern said. Looking confident, he climbed into the front seat of his car. "My contract also states that part of my job at the Air and Space Museum will be to attend community board meetings on the museum's behalf."

"So?" Amal said.

"So it probably seemed like a very minor thing," Mr. Stern continued, "but I've been trying to push through a rezoning of that land for months. As the deciding vote *and* the representative of this museum, that will no longer be a problem."

"And that's the meeting you're heading to right now, isn't it?" Dr. Farah said. "What have I done?"

Mr. Stern laughed and closed the car door. The driver's window slid down. "I'll see you later," he said. "Thanks for helping me pull off the real estate deal of the decade."

"But you can't do that!" Raining protested. "We'll call the police."

Mr. Stern laughed. "Please," he said. "I've broken no laws. In fact I've used the law for every step of my plan."

"Dad, you have to stop him!" Amal exclaimed.

"But I don't—" Dr. Farah paused for a moment, then seemed to realize something. "Wait a moment." He put a hand on the door of the car. "Mr. Stern," he said, smiling, "you're fired."

Mr. Stern stared back at Dr. Farah, a smile frozen on his face. It quickly crumbed into a scowl.

"You can't do that!" Mr. Stern said. "I'll stop payments on the donation check! You'll be stuck with a half-finished, junk wing!"

"Better than no wing at all," Dr. Farah said. "You'll never get your shoddy condos or that ten million dollars in your piggy bank. Goodbye, Mr. Stern. You can mail back your employee ID and parking permit."

CHAPTER 13
Coming Together

"We won't be able to open the new wing without the funds from Mr. Stern's foundation," Dr. Farah said sadly as he led the group of amateur investigators back inside.

"Well," Bridget offered, "I did manage to raise a little money earlier this year when the Art Museum was trying to buy that land from Brave Star."

"If Mr. Stern follows through and cancels the donation," Dr. Farah said, "we'll have to get rid of the land again and save that expense."

"I had another idea," Bridget Byrne said. "Let me just make a few calls."

* * *

It took several months, a few more donations, and some never-before-seen collaboration between the Capitol City Air and Space Museum and the Capitol City Art Museum, but Bridget and Dr. Farah made it happen—with a little help from Clementine and Amal.

"A shared wing," Amal said at the ceremony to begin fixing Mr. Stern's unfinished construction.

"Between our two favorite museums," Clementine said.

"It is brilliant," Bridget said. "If I do say so myself."

Dr. Farah nodded. "A wing that explores where our two passions meet," he said. "Truly inspired." He smiled at Bridget, and she smiled back.

Amal took Clementine by the hand. "I was thinking," she said. "How about a whole display on the science of paint pigments?"

"Ooh, I'd love that," Clementine said. "Or maybe we can get Van Gogh's 'Starry Night' for a special exhibit!"

"Brilliant," Amal said, squeezing Clementine's hand with affection. "Science and art really do work well together."

Steve B.

About the Author

Steve Brezenoff is the author of more than fifty middle-grade chapter books, including the Field Trip Mysteries series, the Ravens Pass series of thrillers, and the Return to Titanic series. In his spare time, he enjoys video games, cycling, and cooking. Steve lives in Minneapolis with his wife, Beth, and their son and daughter.

Lisa W.

About the Illustrator

Lisa K. Weber is an illustrator currently living in Oakland, California. She graduated from Parsons School of Design in 2000, and then began freelancing. Since then she has completed many print, animation, and design projects, including graphic novelizations of classic literature, character and background designs for children's cartoons, and textiles for dog clothing.

GLOSSARY

adjacent (uh-JEY-suhnt)—lying next to or near, with a border or point in common

collaboration (kuh-lab-uh-REY-shuhn)—working together with others

cutthroat (KUHT-throht)—a cruel person with no scruples

doctorate (DOK-ter-it)—the highest degree a person can earn from a college or university

honorary (ON-uh-rer-ee)—given or done as a sign of respect

lectern (LEK-tuhrn)—a stand or desk with a slanted top to holds papers for a person speaking

lunar (LOO-ner)—of, relating to, or resembling the moon

luncheon (LUHN-chuhn)—a light meal at midday, typically held in connection with a meeting or other special occasion

philanthropist (fi-LAN-thruh-pist)—a person who gives time or money to help others

valiant (VAL-yuhnt)—brave or courageous

DISCUSSION QUESTIONS

1. Amal, Raining, Clementine, and Wilson
each have a parent who works at a
museum: the Air and Space Museum,
the American History Museum, the
Art Museum, and the Natural History
Museum. Which museum would you most
like to visit? Discuss your choice.

2. Clementine and Amal get into a fight
when Amal accuses Bridget of being
behind the empty crates. Do you think
Amal was wrong to be mad at Clementine
for taking Bridget's side? If so, why?

3. Mr. Stern makes himself the star of his
new exhibit. What are some signs he's not
very interested in the museum outside of
promoting himself?

WRITING PROMPTS

1. If you could create your own wing at the Air and Space Museum, what would it showcase? Write down a description of your museum wing and make sure to list what would be on display.

2. Bridget admits that it's upsetting when local politicians decide science museums get more money than art museums. Write a letter from Bridget's perspective, explaining why art museums should get as much money as science museums.

3. Amal accuses Bridget without any real proof. Write a letter from Amal's perspective apologizing to Bridget for making her a suspect.

EXPLORING
AIR AND SPACE

In 1976, the Smithsonian's National Air and Space Museum opened in Washington, D.C., with the mission to "commemorate, educate, inspire." The museum was originally intended to focus only on earthbound flight. But in 1966, the museum began to gather artifacts from NASA and added space exploration to its exhibits. (At that point, the Museum's collections were held in the "Tin Shed," a Quonset hut the War Department constructed behind the Smithsonian Castle.)

Today the Smithsonian's National Air and Space Museum is the largest of the Smithsonian's nineteen museums. It's made up of two separate facilities: the Air and Space Museum, in Washington, D.C., and the Steven F. Udvar-Hazy Center in Chantilly, Virginia. The museum houses approximately 60,000 incredible artifacts, including the plane the Wright brothers flew. Together, the two facilities welcome more than eight million people each year, making it the most visited museum in the United States.

TELESCOPES OF TODAY AND TOMORROW

The first telescope that looked at the stars was made by Galileo in 1609. While his telescope wasn't very strong, he was able to see details on the moon.

In the 1970s, NASA and the European Space Agency began working on a telescope that could be sent into space to get more detailed images. Their work launched in 1990, when the first space telescope, the Hubble, was sent into the stars. The Hubble telescope takes pictures of deep space.

The Hubble's successor, the James Webb Space Telescope, is scheduled to be launched into space in the year 2021. It is a highly advanced telescope that NASA hopes will help them get important information about distant galaxies.